Pistols and Politics

Alexander Hamilton Duels Aaron Burr

August Greeley

ROSEN CLASSROOM
PRIMARYSOURCE

Rosen Classroom Books & Materials™

New York

Published in 2004 by The Rosen Publishing Group, Inc.
29 East 21st Street, New York, NY 10010

Editor: Jennifer Silate
Book Design: Christopher Logan
Photo researcher: Rebecca Anguin-Cohen
Series photo researcher: Jeff Wendt

Photo Credits: Cover (right), title page, pp. 6, 22 ; © North Wind Picture Archives; cover (left)
illustration © Debra Wainwright/The Rosen Publishing Group; p. 10 courtesy collections of the New
Jersey Historical Society, Newark, NJ; p. 14 © Culver Pictures; p. 18 © Bettmann/Corbis;
p. 29 © Hulton/Archive/Getty Images; pp. 30, 31, 32 Collection of The New York Historical Society

ISBN: 0-8239-4327-5
6-pack ISBN: 0-8239-4328-3

Manufactured in the United States of America

CONTENTS

Preface

The American Revolutionary War lasted from 1775 to 1783. General George Washington led the American army against the British. Alexander Hamilton and Aaron Burr were Washington's assistants. Hamilton was one of Washington's favorite assistants. Washington and Burr, however, did not get along. Burr worked under Washington for only a couple of months.

When the war was over, it was time to set up the government of the new country. In 1789, George Washington became the first president of the United States. He named Alexander Hamilton to the job of secretary of the treasury. Hamilton worked on a plan to help make the young nation's economy strong.

In 1791, Burr beat Hamilton's father-in-law, General Philip Schuyler in an election for the U.S. Senate. This upset Hamilton because he wanted Schuyler in the Senate to support his economic plans.

During this time, there were two main political parties in the United States—the Federalists and the Republicans. The Federalists wanted a strong national government. The Republicans wanted states to have most of the power. Aaron Burr was a Republican. Alexander Hamilton was a Federalist. In 1800, Thomas Jefferson ran for president of the United States, and Aaron Burr ran for vice president.

In October 1800, Burr published a copy of a paper that Hamilton had written against John Adams. Adams was the president of the United States. Hamilton had not wanted the paper to be made public because Adams was also a Federalist. After the paper was published, members of the Federalist Party argued among themselves over how to run the government and the party. As the November 1800 presidential election came closer, the Republicans gained a lead because of this fighting. Hamilton and Burr were now political enemies.

Alexander Hamilton worked hard to build the United States of America. His ideas have helped the country become what it is today.

Chapter One

BURR'S LOSS

*I*t was February 1801. The voting for president and vice president of the United States was over. Aaron Burr could barely hold in his happiness. He was waiting in his friend, Matthew's house, in Washington, D.C., to find out if he was to be named the new president. Voting rules were different at this time. Burr and Thomas Jefferson had received the same number of votes in the election. Now, either man could be made the president, even though Burr ran for vice president. It was up to Congress to pick which man would win. Burr knew that many of the Federalists hated Jefferson because of his role as head of the Republican Party. He thought he might just win the race.

"Please sit down, Aaron," Matthew said. "If you don't, you'll be too tired to accept the presidency!" The two men laughed nervously.

Another friend, Daniel, cleared his throat. "You may not become president at all," he warned Burr. "Not if Alexander Hamilton has anything to do with it."

Suddenly, Burr's smile disappeared. It was replaced by an angry frown. "Hamilton!" he yelled. "What have you heard?"

"Hamilton has spent all day with congressmen in the Federalist Party," Daniel began. "He has asked them to support Jefferson and not you."

Burr did not wait to hear any more. He grabbed his coat. He headed for the Capitol building to see if what his friend said was true.

Hamilton sat in an office in the newly finished Senate wing of the Capitol building. Though he no longer worked in the government, Hamilton spent much of his time with government workers. He wanted to make sure that the new leaders did not steer the country off course. He rubbed his eyes. He hadn't been getting much sleep. He had talked to congressmen all day to get them to support Jefferson for president over his enemy, Aaron Burr. He did not think that Burr could lead the country. Hamilton believed that Burr was not to be trusted. Hamilton's thoughts were interrupted by a knock at his door.

"Excuse me, Mr. Hamilton," a young man at the door said. "I just wanted to tell you, sir, the final vote has been made," the young man said. "Thomas Jefferson has been elected president of the United States."

Hamilton sat back in his chair. A grin spread across his face. All of his hard work had paid off—Burr had lost the election.

Moments later, Burr arrived at the Capitol building. A few of his friends were in the hallway as he entered. "Has the vote been made?" Burr asked.

"Yes, Aaron," one of his friends said, shaking Burr's hand. "I'm sorry, but Jefferson won. You will only be vice president. Hamilton succeeded in changing a few of the Federalists' minds."

Burr's face turned red. "This is too much. I will get Hamilton for this!" he said as he stormed out of the building.

This painting of Aaron Burr was done in 1794 by Gilbert Stuart. At the time of the painting, Burr and Hamilton's disagreement had already begun.

Chapter Two

THE CHALLENGE

Over the next few years, Hamilton stayed busy. He built a large house for his family in a part of New York City that was still farmland. He called his home The Grange. Some of his friends thought he should leave politics and spend his time raising vegetables in his new garden. After all, he had worked very hard for the United States. They believed it was time he enjoyed the good things he had earned. Hamilton couldn't do that, though. The politics of the country were always on his mind. He even started his own newspaper, the *New York Evening Post*. Hamilton often wrote articles in his paper to share his political views.

Late one evening in early 1804, Hamilton spoke with his newspaper's editor. "Is there still time to put an article in tomorrow's paper?" he asked.

The editor laughed. "Let me guess. You wrote an article against Vice President Burr's run for governor of New York?" he said.

Hamilton nodded. "I won't rest until that man's career is finished. The Republicans won't let him run for president in their party, so he has become a Federalist. But he does not believe in the Federalist Party. He goes where he thinks he can find power. He will run for president again. He must not succeed," he said.

Hamilton's efforts worked: Burr did not win. Burr blamed Hamilton for his loss. He knew that Hamilton had made many speeches insulting his ability to lead. A few days after the election, Burr walked into his office and saw a page from a newspaper lying on his desk. "Who brought this?" Burr asked his assistant, William Van Ness. Van Ness shrugged.

Burr's eyes raced over the article. Each time he finished a sentence, his anger grew. It was an article about Hamilton's last speech before the election. "This time, he has gone too far!"

Burr yelled, crumpling the page in his fist. "Hamilton calls me 'a dangerous man.' He says I am not to be trusted. It is because of him that I lost the election! Does he expect me to ignore these insults?"

"What are you going to do?" Van Ness asked.

Burr tore out the article and put it in an envelope. "Deliver this to Hamilton. Ask him one simple question: Did he say these words or not? If he admits to saying them, demand an apology!"

Van Ness returned with a letter from Hamilton. In it, Hamilton wrote that he *did* say what had been printed in the article. However, he would not apologize for saying it. More letters between the two men followed.

On June 27, Burr wrote a final letter. "Here, take this to him. Let's see what he says now," Burr said as he handed Van Ness the letter. "I've challenged him to a pistol duel. We will settle this once and for all."

Hamilton built his house, the Grange, in 1802. It still stands today in New York City.

Chapter Three

CHALLENGE ACCEPTED

At this time, Hamilton was at his home in New York. He was in his living room with his wife, Betsey, and his nineteen-year-old daughter, Angelica. With them was his assistant, Nathaniel Pendleton. Hamilton, Betsey, and Pendleton were listening to Angelica play the harp when Van Ness delivered the letter.

"What is it, Alexander?" Betsey asked.

Hamilton stared at the letter. After a moment, he looked at his wife. "It is a letter from Aaron Burr. He has challenged me to a duel," he said.

Betsey looked worried. "What are you going to tell him?" she asked.

"I don't know yet, Betsey. But I fear I must accept the challenge," Hamilton answered.

Angelica started crying and ran from the room.

Tears formed in Betsey's eyes. "Why don't you simply tell him no?" she asked.

"There is nothing simple about it, Betsey!" Hamilton snapped. "Don't you understand why I must accept? Great things are at stake here. My political career! My honor!" he added.

Betsey put her head in her hands. "Is your honor worth more than your life?" she sobbed. "We've already lost our son Philip in a duel. I won't lose you, too." With that, Betsey left the room to join her daughter.

Hamilton turned to his assistant. "Tell me, Nathaniel," he said. "Am I as foolish as my wife believes? Should I refuse Burr's challenge?"

"If you accept his challenge, your duel will be against the law in this state," Pendleton replied.

"I know," said Hamilton.

"We will probably have to travel to the shores of New Jersey, to Weehawken," Pendleton said.

"Weehawken," Hamilton said. "That's where Philip was killed."

"Since that day," Pendleton reminded Hamilton, "you have hated duels."

For a long while, Hamilton was silent. He thought of his dead son. It had been three years since Philip lost his life in a duel. Would he suffer the same fate as his son? He thought about his family and about Burr. "My hatred for dishonor is far worse than my hatred for duels," Hamilton whispered. "Tell Burr that I accept his challenge."

"In that case, I will go to Burr's assistant. Perhaps the two of us can find a peaceful end to this matter," Pendleton said.

Hamilton agreed. "Tell his assistant that I do not plan to harm Burr. To prove it, I will throw away my shot," he said. He meant he would fire his pistol harmlessly into the air. This was an honorable way of settling a duel. However, it was also a deadly risk to take: Burr might not be willing to do the same.

Many artists have drawn pictures of what they think happened during Hamilton and Burr's duel. This print shows Hamilton (right) and Burr (left) at the moment before they fire their pistols. Their assistants stand in the background.

Chapter Four

THE DAY OF THE DUEL

T he day of the duel was set for July 11, 1804. That morning, Hamilton and Pendleton boarded a boat to cross the Hudson River from New York to New Jersey. A doctor had joined them for the trip. The sky was cloudless. The sun was hot on Hamilton's neck. As his boat moved downstream, Hamilton quickly looked back toward his home. He thought of his family. Would he ever see Betsey and his children again?

The men were silent for most of the ride. A bird flew just above the water, looking for its first meal of the day. "You told Burr's assistant of my plan?" Hamilton asked suddenly, breaking the silence. Hamilton still planned on throwing his shot away. He would wait for Burr to shoot the first round. Then Hamilton would fire harmlessly into the air.

The assistants would declare the duel over. The men would be able to walk away.

"I told him about your plan," Pendleton replied. "But Burr's assistant has told me that...."

"If Burr is any kind of gentleman," Hamilton interrupted, "the duel will end there. We will lose no honor and no blood."

"Alexander, I must tell you...," Pendleton started.

Hamilton silenced his assistant. He was ready for the duel. He would throw his shot away. Let Burr do what he wanted. Burr was forty-eight years old, one year younger than Hamilton. If Hamilton died, Burr's career would surely be over for good. If he lived, Hamilton could continue his work for his country. Now was not the time for Pendleton's worries.

Pendleton *was* worried, though. He had learned from Van Ness that Burr had been preparing for the duel. After dinner each night, Burr would walk to an open field and fire several practice rounds. *Why would a man who planned on throwing his shot away do that?* he thought.

They arrived at Weehawken, New Jersey, and docked the boat. The men climbed a cliff. Burr and his assistant were already waiting at the top. Pendleton opened the lid to a wooden box he was carrying. Hamilton peered inside and saw his pistol. Pendleton handed it to Hamilton.

The two assistants looked at each other nervously. "We beg you both to put down your weapons," Pendleton said to Burr and Hamilton. "Let's find a way to settle this matter peacefully."

"He will not apologize," Burr said, pointing at Hamilton. "So I will not withdraw my challenge."

The men stood with their backs to each other. Hamilton stood upright. His back brushed against Burr's. They began to walk away from each other. With each step, Hamilton heard his heart thump a bit louder, a bit faster. Finally, the men took their tenth and final step.

"Present!" the assistants yelled out.

The men turned around at this signal. Pistols were drawn. Each man looked sharply at the other. It was time for Hamilton to face his fate, whatever it might be....

This woodcut shows the moment when Burr fired the deadly shot that killed Hamilton.

Chapter Five

THE FINAL SHOT

A shot rang out. Burr's bullet sent Hamilton flying. Pain exploded in Hamilton's side. His spine burned as though it had been set on fire. Hamilton's arms flung upward, and he pulled the trigger on his pistol. A second shot rang out. Hamilton's bullet struck a small tree branch above his head.

"I am a dead man!" Hamilton cried out. With those words, he fell to the ground. His pistol slipped out of his hand. Seconds later, the branch broke off the tree and fell beside him. Leaves from the tree flew everywhere. A few fell on Hamilton's face. A breeze carried others away.

Hamilton could smell the gun smoke rising from his open wound. One moment he was awake and in pain. The next, he was asleep and in peace. He wondered why he should even bother waking at all. Suddenly, he felt hands grabbing him. Someone was tearing off his jacket. He heard his friends talking.

"He is bleeding heavily," the doctor said.

"Can you help him?" asked Pendleton.

"The bullet has torn through his liver. We have to move him quickly," the doctor answered.

"We should go to Mr. Worthington's in Manhattan," Pendleton said.

"Let's go, then," the doctor said. "There's no time to lose."

"How bad is it?" Pendleton asked.

The doctor lifted Hamilton's blood-soaked shirt and looked at the wound. "It may be deadly," he said.

Once they reached the Worthingtons' house, Pendleton placed Hamilton on a bed. The doctor got right to work. He was able to wake Hamilton. However, Hamilton could not sit up on his own. The bullet had gone deep into his spine. Because of this, he had lost all feeling in his legs. Hamilton looked around the strange room. He asked Pendleton to write down his last words. "I do not hate Burr for doing this to me," he began. "I hope he knows this. I forgive Burr for his actions. My hope is that he proves himself worthy of honor after I am gone."

Pendleton dipped his pen into an inkwell. As he wrote, he didn't want to doubt that his friend was being truthful. But as he listened to Hamilton's final words, he thought perhaps—just perhaps— Hamilton was still trying to get back at Burr. Burr may have won the duel, but the war between he and Hamilton had lasted for years. Why should Hamilton give up now? Why not try to make the public angry with Burr? That way, Hamilton could win one last war against him. Pendleton pushed these thoughts from his mind as he finished his final job for Hamilton.

That afternoon, Hamilton took a turn for the worse. He cried out in pain. He passed out for several minutes. Moments later, Betsey along with Hamilton's children entered the room. They had left home the moment they heard he had been shot. Hamilton kissed his wife. He lived through the night, but was still near death. Alexander Hamilton died at 2:00 P.M. on July 12, 1804.

When the news of Hamilton's death was made public, many people turned against Burr—and dueling. Burr became wanted for murder in New Jersey and New York. Burr moved to Pennsylvania. He became one of the first people to be charged with murder after a duel. However, he did not go to jail. Burr continued to serve as vice president until his term was over in 1805. After his vice presidency, Burr tried unsuccessfully to take over Mexico and start a new government there. When President Jefferson found out about his plan, Burr was arrested. Though Burr was not found guilty of treason, he was not trusted by many. Burr went to Europe. Eventually, he returned to New York and worked as a lawyer. He died at the age of eighty on September 14, 1836.

The famous duel that left a bloody mark on American history took one man's life and ended another's career. These terrible events made Americans realize that pistols and politics don't mix.

Glossary

apology (uh-POL-uh-jee) an admission that you are sorry about something

duel (DOO-uhl) a fight between two people using swords or guns, fought according to strict rules

economic (ee-kuh-NOM-ik) based on the way money, goods, and services are made and used in a society

insult (in-SUHLT) to say or do something rude and upsetting to somebody

lawyer (LAW-yur) a person who is trained to advise people about the law and who acts and speaks for them in court

pistol (PISS-tuhl) a small gun designed to be held in the hand

politics (POL-uh-tiks) the debate and activity involved in governing a country

publish (PUHB-lish) to produce and distribute a book, magazine, newspaper, or any other printed material so that people can buy it

treason (TREE-zuhn) the crime of betraying your country by spying for another country or by helping an enemy during a war

PRIMARY SOURCES

How do we know about the events of Alexander Hamilton's life that took place two hundred years ago? Studying materials, such as letters, diaries, maps, and paintings, can give us some clues. These clues help us learn about historical events as well as people who lived in the past. The letter on page 30 is one of these clues. It is from Aaron Burr to Alexander Hamilton. By reading the letter, we can identify the strong feelings Aaron Burr had against Hamilton in their ongoing feud.

Newspaper articles also give details about the past. When we analyze the article that appears on page 31, we better understand the public's feelings about Alexander Hamilton's death.

Objects also help us understand the past. By studying the fancy and costly engravings on the dueling pistols shown on page 29, we can draw the conclusion that dueling was done mainly among rich people. Only they would be likely to afford such expensive guns. Clues such as these help tell us about the people, places, and events of the past.

Dueling was very common in the early 1800s. Many people owned dueling pistols, like the ones pictured here.

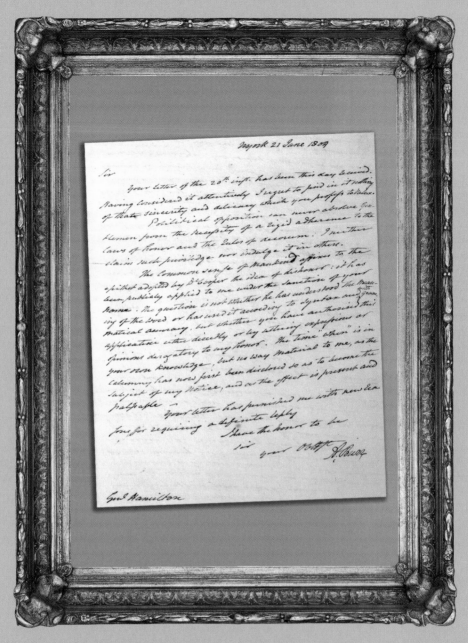

In this letter, dated June 21, 1804, Aaron Burr angrily responds to a letter from Alexander Hamilton. In the letter, Burr asks if Hamilton said that Burr had no honor.

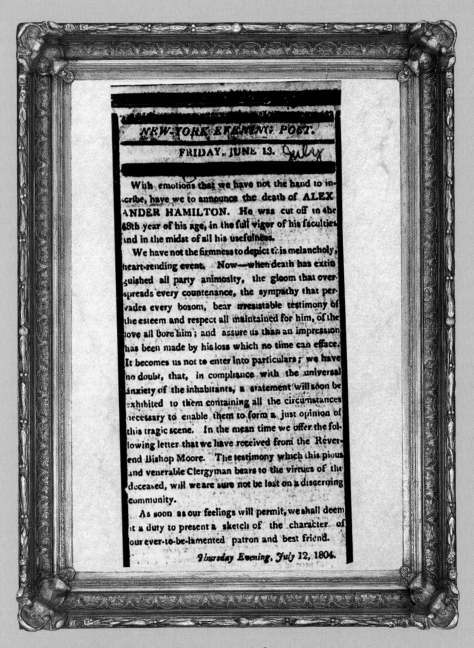

NEW-YORK EVENING POST.

FRIDAY, JUNE 13. *July*

With emotions that we have not the hand to inscribe, have we to announce the death of ALEXANDER HAMILTON. He was cut off in the 48th year of his age, in the full vigor of his faculties, and in the midst of all his usefulness.

We have not the firmness to depict this melancholy, heart-rending event. Now—when death has extinguished all party animosity, the gloom that overspreads every countenance, the sympathy that pervades every bosom, bear irresistable testimony of the esteem and respect all maintained for him, of the love all bore him; and assure us than an impression has been made by his loss which no time can efface. It becomes us not to enter into particulars; we have no doubt, that, in compliance with the universal anxiety of the inhabitants, a statement will soon be exhibited to them containing all the circumstances necessary to enable them to form a just opinion of this tragic scene. In the mean time we offer the following letter that we have received from the Reverend Bishop Moore. The testimony which this pious and venerable Clergyman bears to the virtues of the deceased, will we are sure not be lost on a discerning community.

As soon as our feelings will permit, we shall deem it a duty to present a sketch of the character of our ever-to-be-lamented patron and best friend.

Thursday Evening, July 12, 1804.

News of Hamilton's death spread fast. Hamilton's newspaper, the *New York Evening Post* published the news of his death on July 13, 1804.

Betsey Hamilton lived for another fifty years after her husband's death.